The Bulliest Dozer

Eric Fehr
Pamela Duncan Edwards

Illustrated By Kate Komarnicki

On the day that his mom and dad began new jobs in the area,
Bo Dozer joined Ms. Crane's Academy for Little Machines.
"Let's all make Bo feel welcome," said Ms. Crane.

"Do you want to give out the cookies with me at snack time?" asked Lofty Forklift.

"Do you want to borrow my best pencil?" asked Chippie Hedge Trimmer.

"Do you want to play tag at recess?" asked Whippy Weedwacker.

"I'll save a place for you at lunch," promised Wobbles Wheelbarrow.

"I'll let you share my grass-and-dandelion sandwich," offered Mow Garden Tractor.

That afternoon, they all went to the rink to practice a Holiday-Concert-on-Ice for their parents. Windy Leafblower and Crush Garbage-Truck tried to show Bo how to skate but his tracks got jumbled.

Bo snow-ploughed
down the rink.

He slipped and slid.

He fell over.

He nose-dived into one side
and skidded into the other.

He blushed bright red as Ms. Crane
helped him off the ice.

"You'll do better next
time," she promised.

When Bo tried to tell his parents about his awful afternoon, they were too busy and tired to listen.

"Could we go to the rink on Saturday so I can practice?" asked Bo.

"Sorry," said his mom. "Dad's working and I'm having my track polish changed to orange so it won't clash with the fall leaves."

THIS MADE BO SAD!

IT MADE BO MAD!

SO BO DECIDED TO ACT OUT-**BIG TIME!**

BO BECAME ...

A MEAN MACHINE!

Bo tripped Lofty Forklift into
a puddle and made him cry.
"Baby! Baby! Cry Baby!"
mocked Bo.

He popped Crush
Garbage-Truck's
'HAPPY BIRTHDAY'
balloon.

He broke Chippie
Hedge Trimmer's
best pencil.

He teased Wobbles
Wheelbarrow.
"You're not a
real machine,"
he scoffed.
"You don't even
have a motor."

He spilled milk all over Mow's grass-and-dandelion sandwich.

"That might make your yucky lunch taste
better," he giggled.

"You're so THIN," he said to
Whippy Weedwacker.
"If you put a light on top of
your head, you'd look like
a street lamp."

Bo jammed a trashcan under the doorknob when Windy went to the girls' bathroom. Whippy had to rescue her. Every day, Bo teased and teased. "He's the BULLIEST DOZER EVER," they all agreed.

No matter
how many times he
tried, Bo's skating didn't
improve. But no one dared help
because they were scared of him.

I'm useless, thought Bo. So he decided
to stop practicing. Of course, his skating
got worse and worse.

This made him madder than ever.

Soon everybody began to spread out on the lunch benches. They didn't want to sit with Bo. Bo pretended he didn't care. But he did.

When they played soccer, he was always last to be chosen. No one wanted to be on the same team as Bo. Bo pretended he didn't care. But he did.

When they walked in a line, nobody wanted to be near Bo.
Bo pretended he didn't care. But he did.

His parents were too busy to notice him
and now he'd lost his new friends, too.

On the morning of the concert, the little machines began to panic.

"What if he hides my skates?" said Crush.

"If he unties my skate lace, I'll wobble over," wailed Wobbles.

"What if he trips me up again?" worried Lofty.

"Should we tell Ms. Crane?" shouted Whippy.
"YES!" cried everyone. So they did.

Ms. Crane told them not to worry.
She would sort things out.

"Your parents will be sad if you spoil the concert, Bo," said Ms. Crane.
"I bet they won't come," sniffed Bo. "They'll be working or Mom will be at the beauty salon. Anyway, I'm hopeless at skating."

Bo began to cry. “Everyone hates me,” he sobbed.
“So being a bully wasn’t a good idea after all?” said Ms. Crane.
“Guess not,” mumbled Bo, and he hung his head.

But as Ms. Crane got up to give Bo a hug, she saw a curtain of sparkling white climbing up her study window. “Oh, no!” she cried. “How will we get to the rink? The concert will be ruined!”

Bo stared out at the snow. Then he wiped away his tears. “It’s okay, Ms. Crane,” he said quietly. “Leave everything to me. I know what to do.”

"Machines to the rescue!" cried Bo, rushing back to the classroom. "We've got to save our concert! Everybody follow me!"

Bo gave them each a job.

Then he went bulldozing
all the way from the school
to the rink. He came zig-zagging
back again.

"Perfect!" he cried as Mow packed
snow into the sides of the path.

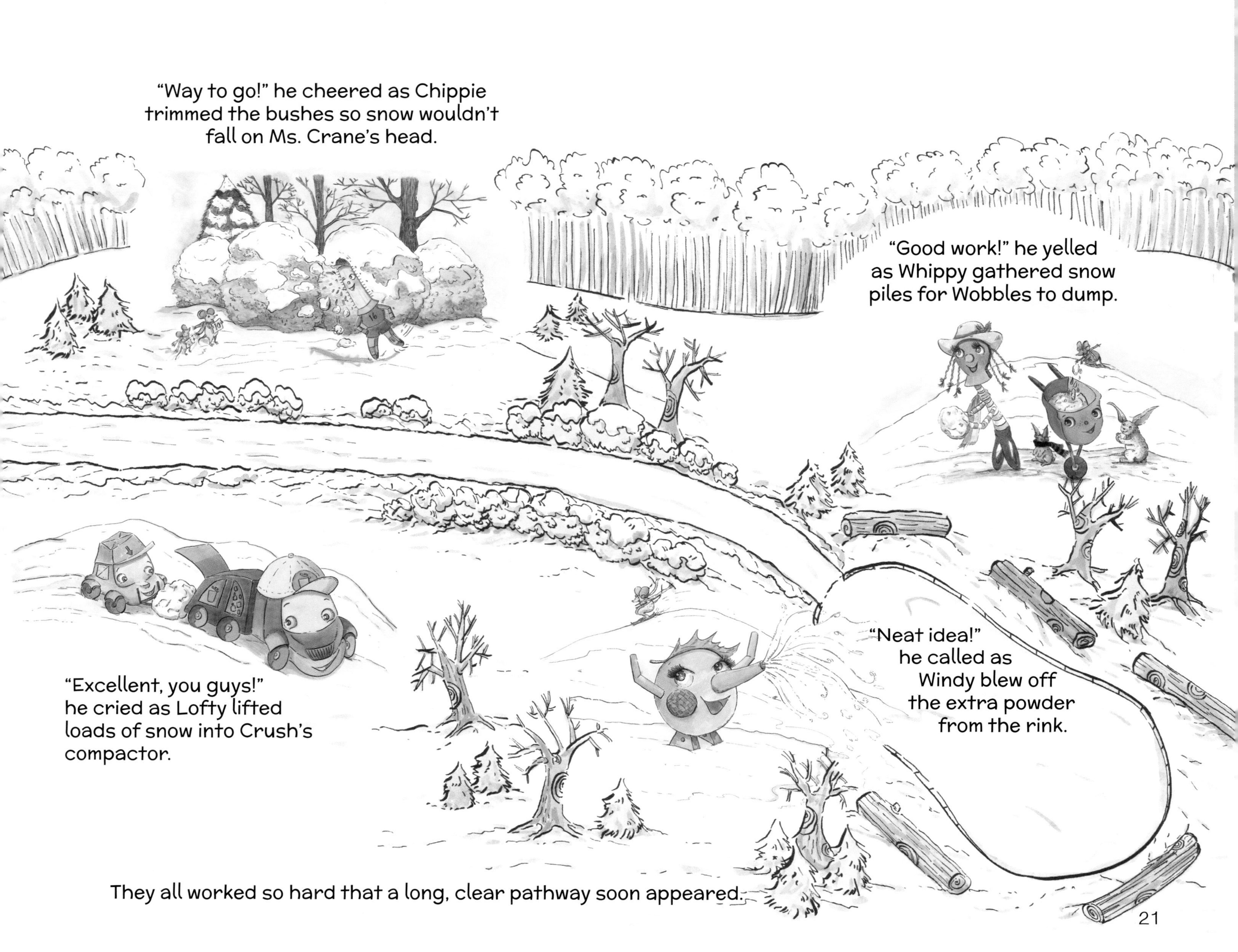

"Way to go!" he cheered as Chippie trimmed the bushes so snow wouldn't fall on Ms. Crane's head.

"Good work!" he yelled as Whippy gathered snow piles for Wobbles to dump.

"Excellent, you guys!" he cried as Lofty lifted loads of snow into Crush's compactor.

"Neat idea!" he called as Windy blew off the extra powder from the rink.

They all worked so hard that a long, clear pathway soon appeared.

After the last bit of snow was cleared,
the little machines gathered around Bo.
"You were GREAT!" they cried.

Bo's face went red. "You guys are the best," he mumbled. "I'm sorry I was a bully. Will you be my friends again?"

"Okay!" they cried. Then off they went to get ready for the concert.

It was the best concert ever.
They skated so perfectly
they could have been ice
hockey players.

All except Bo.

Bo twisted.

Bo spun around on his rear end with
his tracks whirling in the air.

Bo did the splits.

The audience began to clap.
"He's SO funny," they cheered. Bo couldn't believe his ears.
Everyone was cheering for HIM!

Bo saw his mom and dad in the front row waving madly.
They'd come after all.

"YOU'RE A STAR!" they called. "WE'RE PROUD OF YOU!"

"Make a circle," called Bo.
Then Ms. Crane played the piano and
everyone rocked in time to the music.

"We thought we'd have to cancel," cried the little machines. "But Bo saved us."

"He got us to clear a path to the rink," yelled Chippie.

"We couldn't have done it without him," shouted Lofty.

BO BLUSHED BRIGHT RED AGAIN.
BUT HE DIDN'T MIND.
THIS TIME, HE DIDN'T FEEL ASHAMED.
HE FELT WARM AND LOVED.

IF YOU ARE BEING TEASED OR BULLIED AT SCHOOL, HERE ARE SOME THINGS YOU SHOULD DO:

1. Remember that it's not your fault.

2. Ask the bully to stop.

3. Tell your teacher, your school nurse, counselor or another adult in charge.

4. Tell your parents or whomever you live with.

5. Keep as far away from the person teasing you as possible.

6. DON'T BE A BULLY YOURSELF.

IF SOMETHING IS HAPPENING IN YOUR LIFE THAT IS MAKING YOU WORRIED OR SAD, HERE ARE SOME THINGS YOU SHOULD DO:

1. Talk to your teacher, your school nurse, counselor or another adult in charge. Ask them to help you with your problem.

2. Tell your parents or whomever you live with.

3. Don't become a bully yourself. This won't solve your problems.

NO ONE LIKES A BULLY.

With grateful thanks to Dr. Debra Jersin Lane for sharing her invaluable expertise in the problem of bullying in schools. With Love, PDE.

To my ever-loving and supportive wife, Rachel. I'd be lost without you!
And to my beautiful daughter, Elle, whose smile lights up my world. With love always: EF

To Dana Dembeck and Beth Carnill who have given me such generous help, support and friendship. With love, PDE

To all my friends and family who believed in me, and especially Josh. With love, KK

In this story a little bulldozer learns that being a bully doesn't pay.
But by putting his own talents to use when a crisis hits his school, he finds happiness and friends.

1. Machines – Fiction. 2. Bullying. 3. Humorous stories. 4. Ice-Skating.

ISBN: 978-0-6922133-9-1